M000033478

Lady Hathaway's Indecent Proposal

A Hathaway Heirs Novella

SUZANNA MEDEIROS

Copyright © 2013 Saozinha Medeiros

All rights reserved.

ISBN-13: 9780991823758

This is a work of fiction. Names, characters, places, and incidents are the product of the author's imagination or are used fictitiously. Any resemblance to actual events, locales, or persons, living or dead, is purely coincidental.

OTHER BOOKS BY SUZANNA

Dear Stranger

Landing a Lord series
Dancing with the Duke
Loving the Marquess
Beguiling the Earl—coming soon

Hathaway Heirs
Lady Hathaway's Indecent Proposal
Lord Hathaway's New Bride—coming soon

DEDICATION

To all my writing friends, who are too numerous to list. Thank you for your inspiration and support over the years.

CONTENTS

CHAPTER ONE

UNTIL THAT MORNING the Earl of Sanderson would have said he was long past making a fool of himself for Miranda Hathaway, yet here he was, following her butler into the drawing room of her London town house. He told himself it was only curiosity that led him to accept her request for a meeting. After all, they hadn't seen one another in twelve years, so why on earth would she want to see him now?

He took in the room's ornate furnishings as the butler bowed and left to fetch his mistress. Viscount Hathaway had always made a point of displaying his vast wealth at every opportunity, as was evidenced by the amount of gilt in the room. He wondered if Miranda approved of the decor, or if she, too, found it lacking in taste. The old Miranda would have believed the latter. Or so he'd thought at the time, but that was before she'd broken it off with him to marry the much wealthier older man.

Unease settled in the pit of his stomach, and annoyed at the sign of weakness, he moved to the window and looked out onto the fashionable Mayfair neighborhood. It was early for a social call and the road was quiet. No doubt most of Miranda's neighbors were still abed, recovering from whatever entertainments had kept them up the evening before. He would have been sleeping as well if Miranda's message hadn't arrived last night before he'd left for his club.

He resisted the urge to turn around and leave, just as she had done that last time they'd seen one another. Once again, he was at a disadvantage with her. In her house, at her summons, no knowledge of what this meeting was about. He was not, however, the same untried youth he'd been back then. If Miranda assumed so, she would be more than a little surprised.

He sensed her approach and turned in time to see her enter the room. He couldn't help but notice she still moved with the same grace she'd possessed as a young woman, setting the *ton* ablaze during her first season with her beauty and unaffected charm. It had been inevitable that she'd captured his interest as well. But the new widow standing across the room from him now, clad in stark black, was far different from the girl of eighteen who'd worn only pale colors.

That was a lifetime ago.

"My lord," she said, executing a fluid curtsey. Her expression gave no hint as to why she had sent for him.

He inclined his head in acknowledgement and watched in silence as she sat on one end of the ornate settee. A chair was positioned at an angle from her and it was clear she expected him to use it.

A need to ruffle her impassive bearing had him remaining silent and ignoring the chair. He moved past her and sat, instead, beside her on the settee. He left a respectable distance between them, but the way she stiffened told him she hadn't expected him to sit so close. It was self-indulgent, but he felt a small measure of triumph at her discomfort.

He watched, more than a little surprised, as she

collected herself, smoothing away all signs of discomfort. Her body relaxed, her expression becoming one of polite cordiality as she held herself with an almost unnatural stillness. It appeared Miranda Hathaway had learned to control the youthful exuberance she'd once possessed. He wasn't sure whether to applaud her for her newfound reserve or mourn the loss of that once vibrant, impetuous young woman.

Silence stretched between them for several seconds before she turned to face him. He was struck once again, as he had been all those years ago, by her beauty. Her dark brown hair and the unrelieved black of her dress called attention to her pale coloring, making it seem as though she were carved from ivory. Her gray eyes were larger than he remembered, but she was also much thinner than when he'd known her. Almost painfully so. He almost asked if she was well but resisted the impulse. He had no desire to hear about how much she mourned the loss of the husband whose funeral had been only the week before.

The curve of her breasts and her unfashionably plump mouth were the only things about her that were still full. His eyes flickered downward and he remembered with unexpected vividness just how those full lips had felt under his. He'd been with many other women since they'd parted ways, but he'd never enjoyed kissing anyone as much as he had Miranda. Thoughts of how she could put that mouth to another use sent a wave of unwelcome heat through him.

He'd miscalculated. He'd wanted to set Miranda off balance, but being this close to her was having an unwanted effect on him.

"Thank you for accepting my invitation," she said, cutting through the uncomfortable silence. "I know it is early, but I can ring for tea if you haven't eaten yet this morning."

His wayward thoughts under control, he met her emotionless gaze with one of his own. "I think we can dispense with the niceties. We both know this isn't a social call."

Those luscious lips tilted ever so slightly at the corners. "I see you are still as direct as always."

"And I can see you've taken to hiding behind social conventions. You were never one to dance around a subject. You asked me to visit and, despite my reservations, I came. You clearly have something you wish to discuss with me."

He was surprised when she stood.

"This was a mistake." She took a step toward the doorway. "Forgive me for inconveniencing you."

After a brief moment of hesitation, he rose from the settee and moved to block her path. She stopped but kept her eyes averted.

"Miranda."

She didn't move. Against his better judgment, he placed a hand under her chin and tilted her face up to his. They stood that way for several long moments, during which he was painfully aware of the small woman before him. The woman who, he now knew, still had the power to make him want her. She, on the other hand, had the appearance of a cornered, frightened animal.

He dropped his hand and kept his voice even, sensing she was a hairsbreadth away from bolting. "Why did you wish to see me?"

She hesitated and then he saw the resolve form in her eyes.

"Very well," she said before taking a step back.

She moved around him to the door, and this time he didn't stop her—he knew she wouldn't attempt to escape again. He expected her to ring for the tea she'd offered him and was taken aback when she closed the door and turned to face him again.

He raised an eyebrow in question but said nothing. She leaned back against the door for a moment before straightening and looking at him directly. Just as she used to do.

"You are aware my husband passed away last week."

"Yes," he said simply. "Please accept my condolences."

He should have offered them when she'd first come into the room, but after a nod of acknowledgment, she continued as though she hadn't noticed his breach in manners.

"The reason I asked you here has to do with his passing."

"Oh? I'll admit I have no idea why you'd want to see me."

Her smile was fleeting. "No, of course not."

She moved back to the settee and lowered herself onto it. This time when he followed, he didn't repeat his mistake of sitting next to her. But if she guessed at his reason for choosing the chair, she showed no sign of it.

"There is no delicate way to say this, so I must be blunt."

Her words, as well as her resolute manner, sent every one of his senses into high alert. He wasn't sure if she was aware she'd used those same words all those years ago when she'd told him she was marrying someone else. He was starting to regret preventing her from leaving the room.

"With my husband's nephew due to inherit the entirety of his estate, I will have to rely on his generosity in future."

Andrew had stayed as far away as possible from Hathaway—had tried not to think about him outside of those times he'd had to see him in the House of Lords—so he had no way of knowing if he'd ever met the man's heir.

"Given how important Hathaway's wealth was to you and your parents, surely you don't expect me to believe provisions for your future weren't made before your marriage."

She didn't react to the sarcasm in his tone. "I won't need to resort to begging in the street. But no one imagined I wouldn't provide my husband with an heir, so the settlement outlined for that eventuality is a small one." She hesitated and her eyes slid away from his before she continued. "I have spoken to our solicitor and he informs me that in cases where the widow is still of childbearing years, it is customary to wait a few months to ensure there is no heir on the way."

He couldn't stop his gaze from moving to her abdomen, but given the loose fit of her gown, it was impossible to see if it concealed a small bump. The wave of bitterness that rose at her words caught him off guard.

"I fail to see what this has to do with me."

He started to stand, but she reached across the small space that separated them and laid a hand on his knee. Her touch froze him to the spot and his awareness of the intimacy of their current situation intensified.

She moved back and clasped her hands sedately in her lap, but she hadn't been quick enough to keep him from seeing the telltale tremble in her fingers. "I am not with child," she said as though nothing of import had just happened, "but I am hoping that will not be the case for long."

His mind was still on the unwanted rush of desire her touch had elicited, and so it took him several seconds before he realized what she was suggesting. Air rushed out of his lungs as the full implication of her words hit him. Why she'd summoned him here so early when no one would be about in the street to see his arrival. Why she'd closed the door to make sure the servants wouldn't overhear their conversation.

He welcomed the anger that rose swiftly within him, but he refused to let her see it. He wouldn't give her the satisfaction of knowing she could command more than polite curiosity from him.

"I am afraid I still do not know what any of this has to do with me. I am sure your solicitor would be able to advise you much better than I."

A hint of frustration crossed her face before she masked it. Despite her attempt to appear detached and businesslike, the revealing expression told him she was more emotionally invested in their conversation than she wanted him to know.

"You were never one to be so obtuse, Andrew."

"You will excuse me, Lady Hathaway, if I ask for some of that bluntness you promised me."

Her control was slipping, for this time he clearly saw her wince when he'd used her title. The narrowing of her eyes was minute, but she hadn't been able to hide it. She didn't speak for several long moments, long enough for him to think he had won. He was surprised, therefore, when she straightened, drew back her shoulders and met his gaze squarely.

"I want to have a child and I would like you to be the father of that child."

Disbelief almost robbed him of words. When he opened his mouth to tell her exactly what he thought of her proposal, she continued, forestalling him.

"I am under no illusion that we can continue our former relationship. I will make no demands of you and no one will know the child is yours."

Disappointment tinged the anger burning within him as she spoke. The deceitful, conniving woman sitting before him now, the one who would blithely make plans to defraud the heir to her husband's estate of his rightful inheritance, bore no resemblance whatsoever to the woman he'd once known and loved.

And with that realization came the certainty that he was well and truly free of the hold she had once held over him.

He started to refuse, but something held him back. He might no longer love Miranda, but he couldn't deny that he was still very attracted to her. And despite everything, this new woman sitting before him was a mystery he found himself longing to unravel.

"Can you have children? In twelve years you should have already had more than one."

She didn't hesitate before replying. "Robert was older. Our marriage was not a physical one."

He scoffed at that. "I hope you're not about to tell me you're a virgin."

She closed her eyes for a moment and it seemed as though his question had embarrassed her. Given her former bravado and what she had just asked of him, her reluctance to discuss the details surrounding her outrageous plan was more than a little out of place.

"No. In the beginning he visited me, but it was not long before he stopped."

"Why?"

Annoyance flashed across her face.

"How would I know why? I assumed he had a mistress, but I was not about to ask him."

He couldn't keep himself from asking the obvious question. "How long has it been?"

She looked back at him. "Long enough that I am certain I am not carrying his child."

Her answer was far from satisfactory, but since he didn't want to hear the intimate details of her marriage, he didn't press her further.

They sat there for some time, holding each other's gaze, but neither one willing to make the next move. As the silence lengthened, his awareness of Miranda grew. Images of the two of them in bed, his hands sliding over every inch of her body, her face contorted in ecstasy as she found release, crowded his mind.

He didn't love Miranda, but he still wanted her. Perhaps he wanted to punish her as well. Give her a taste of all she had cast aside when she'd casually dismissed him for a larger fortune.

His lust for her wrestled with his conscience, but in the end it was his desire that won out, and he knew he would give her the affair she wanted. It would, of necessity, be of brief duration if she wanted to pass off his bastard as Hathaway's heir. And God help his black soul, but the thought gave him a sense of grim satisfaction. He'd have his revenge on Miranda, ruin her for any other man, and even the score with Hathaway for stealing the woman he'd so desperately wanted all those years ago.

If she wanted him to do this, however, she would have to work for it. She might have had everything she'd ever wanted fall neatly into her lap, but he was no longer willing to exert himself just because she crooked a finger in his direction.

"Satisfy my curiosity about something," he said, breaking the now oppressive silence. "Why me? I'm sure there are any number of men who would be willing to lie between your legs."

Her face heated at his deliberate crudeness, but he had to admire the fact that she didn't lose her composure.

"I know most men have no problem bedding whichever woman happens to be near at hand at the moment. I was young when I married, however, and have spent most of the last few years at our estate in Northampton. I never learned to be as casual as some women are about their bed partners. And…"

For a moment Andrew would have sworn she looked uncertain. Vulnerable. But clearly that could never be said about a woman who planned to pass off another man's child as the heir to a well-established title.

"And what?" he prompted when she showed no signs of continuing.

"You were once kind to me."

That was a vast understatement if ever he'd heard one. "Yes, well, kindness is the very last thing I feel for you now."

She said nothing to that. What was there to say?

"Did you want to start here or should we go up to your bedroom?"

That got a reaction. Her hand fluttered to her

chest. "I'm not sure. Do you think it would be wise?"

She licked her lips, a gesture, he remembered, that always indicated she was nervous. His groin tightened. He'd been trying to shock her, but it appeared she was quite willing to carry through with her proposition, and his body responded eagerly.

Irritated she could still so easily rouse his desire, he lashed out at her. "Tell me, Miranda, did Hathaway kiss you and caress you before fucking you? Or did he simply raise your nightgown and grunt away on top of you while you congratulated yourself on the excellent match you'd made?"

She didn't try to hide the anger his words had roused. Good, he thought. This was the Miranda he wanted. The calculating, aggressive Miranda. He wanted no reminders of how young and innocent she'd once been.

In reply, she stood. His innate manners had him beginning to stand, but she placed her hands on his shoulders to stop him. He leaned back in the chair and waited to see what she would do next. He wasn't disappointed.

She lowered herself onto his lap, leaned into him, and raised her hands to frame his face. He could feel the rapid rise and fall of her breasts against his chest and, in anticipation, his own breath quickened to match hers. She placed her mouth against his, and in that moment he wanted nothing more than to crush her against him and take what she so freely offered. Instead, he willed himself to remain still, letting her take the lead. She moved her mouth against his, but it soon became clear she'd acted out of bravado and not experience.

When she drew back again, frustration had etched little lines above her nose. Despite the fact she had given him little more than a chaste kiss, she was not unaffected. Her gray eyes had darkened and her breathing was ragged. Aside from confirming the type of marital relations she'd shared with her husband, her kiss had given him another piece of vital information. He needed more, and he needed it now.

When he stood, taking her with him, she gave a surprised gasp and wrapped her arms around his neck. He moved the two steps to the settee and lowered the two of them onto it. She remained on his lap, but now his arms were around her. Her eyes widened when she felt his erection pressing against her hip.

"Right, no kissing," he said, surprised to find his voice hoarse with his effort at controlling himself. "Let me show you how it's done."

He claimed her mouth slowly at first. Touching his lips to hers and brushing them against hers in slow, tantalizing movements aimed at gaining her trust. It was not too dissimilar from the way she had kissed him, but she obviously took comfort from the fact he was now participating. She relaxed against him and the heat of her body, pressed against his, fueled his desire.

He'd been all too innocent and eager to prove himself worthy of her when he'd courted her as a youth and so hadn't kissed her the way he'd longed to. But now, with the confidence that came from experience, he intended to make up for his former restraint. When she sighed, he took advantage of the opportunity to deepen the kiss, tracing his tongue first against her lips and then entering her mouth. She stiffened, but only for a moment before matching his movement.

The notion entered his mind that perhaps she'd been acting the innocent earlier, but he dismissed the notion as inconsequential. Did it really matter? He leaned back against the cushions and she followed, draping her body over his. He groaned as the kiss became more urgent, their tongues and mouths dueling for dominance. Blind to everything but the lust sweeping through him, he placed one hand on her backside and ground his erection against her hip. He lifted his other hand to cup her breast. She moaned low, arching into his touch as he covered her full breast and teased the hardened nipple with his thumb. She moved now, writhing against him. Without conscious thought, he shifted, reversing their positions so that she lay under him on the settee.

When he had her exactly where he wanted, he started to raise her skirts so he could settle between her legs. It took him a few moments to realize that her hands had moved from clinging to his shoulders to trying to push him away.

He lifted his head and looked down at her. Her lips were swollen from their heated kiss and a flush stained her cheeks and upper chest a rosy pink. She was clearly aroused. Behind the heat in her eyes, however, he detected a hint of uncertainty. Damn. How had he lost control so quickly? He closed his eyes, and took a deep breath before pushing himself away from her. He watched in silence as she struggled with her skirts before rising to sit on the other end of the settee. One hand moved to touch her bottom lip and he knew with certainty that neither her husband, nor any other man, had ever kissed her that way.

"Are you…" Flustered, she stopped before starting again. "Does this mean you agree to my request?"

Mere agreement was laughable when compared to the feelings warring within him. Desire. Lust. An almost desperate need to throw her back down and finish what they'd started. Oh yes, he would most definitely give her what she wanted. And at the same time he'd finally get Miranda Hathaway out of his system and be done with her. And if a child resulted… Well, he wouldn't be the first man with a bastard. And in his case he knew his son would be well provided for as the next Viscount Hathaway. And a daughter would also ensure Miranda had claims to the next Viscount's generosity.

Schooling his features to mask his anticipation, he rose and moved to the door. With one hand on the knob he turned back to face her.

"I'll send word of where and when."

At her nod he opened the door and, anxious to be away from Miranda and his newly aroused need for her, showed himself out.

SUZANNA MEDEIROS

CHAPTER TWO

Andrew's note came the following morning. It contained simply an address and a time later that evening and was signed with an *S* for his title— Sanderson. That formality told her everything. He wanted her to know that despite the heated kiss they had shared the previous morning, there was to be no real intimacy between them.

That kiss had haunted her the rest of the day and had led to a night of passionate dreams. It had also served to make her feel like a fraud when acquaintances and family friends called on her to offer their condolences and see how she was faring. While she appreciated their show of support, the very last thing she needed was to be forced to act the part of the grieving widow when all she could think about was the fact she would soon be physically intimate with Andrew.

The hours crawled by and when evening finally arrived, a swarm of butterflies had taken up permanent residence low in her belly. But despite her nerves, she could hardly wait for the appointed hour to arrive. Her brief meeting with Andrew had told her what she had always suspected—there was more to the intimate relations between a man and a woman than what she had experienced in her marriage. She knew men took great pleasure in that physical act, and if the way she'd felt when Andrew had touched her was any indication, she suspected there could also be great pleasure for a woman.

When it was time to prepare for their encounter, she took great care to dress to her best advantage, choosing an outfit that would give her the confidence she'd need. Given the illicit nature of the errand she was on, she couldn't bring herself to wear one of her mourning gowns. She chose, instead, a satin gown of deep red that had a simple row of buttons up the back that she could reach herself with a little effort.

Her maid had been surprised when Miranda dismissed her after the woman had laced her corset, but it was vital that the servants believe she was going out to have a quiet dinner at the home of a family friend. If gossip started to spread about her activities, she would not be able to carry out her supposed ruse and Andrew would have no reason to see her. If that happened, she would never find another reason to entice him to make love with her.

She left her hair in the simple knot her maid had created that morning and concealed her outfit with a black cloak before stepping out into the street. Her butler had been aghast when she'd told him she planned to walk, alone, to her destination, but it was only a few minutes away and he'd had no choice but to acquiesce to her insistence that she be alone. She'd felt a stab of guilt knowing he'd only backed down because he hadn't wanted to upset her further during what was supposed to be a very painful time for her.

To ensure no one would discover her true destination, she hired her first carriage a few blocks from her home and changed hansoms twice during her journey. When the third cab finally stopped at the address Andrew had provided, she was relieved to find herself at a small house on the outskirts of London.

She paid the driver and stepped down from the carriage. Despite her nerves, she thought she'd managed to push aside the last of her misgivings. But standing before the front door of the nondescript house, she couldn't help but wonder if she was making a mistake.

Her husband had been ill for some time, but his illness hadn't been a fatal one. After the shock of Robert's unexpected death the week before had worn off, she'd been taken aback by how quickly the idea for her current plan had come to her. She'd tried to ignore it at first, but the need to see Andrew again, to recapture the emotions she'd once experienced when they had courted, wouldn't leave her.

Their courtship hadn't ended well and it had been her fault. He'd been so young and earnest then, only a year older than her own eighteen years. They'd been in love. She might have been young and inexperienced, but she'd known he would never leave her and she'd felt the same devotion to him. Her confidence that they could have a future together had withered under her parents' displeasure. Andrew had been next in line to be the Earl of Sanderson, but theirs was not a wealthy estate and everyone had expected it would be many years before he came into his modest inheritance. Her parents had, therefore, taken it upon themselves to promise her hand in marriage to the much older Viscount Hathaway.

She couldn't blame them for all that followed. They'd acted in what they considered to be her best interests and she'd relented. She knew in Andrew's eyes it did not speak well to her character that she'd so easily acquiesced to her parents' desires.

And it hadn't been a horrible marriage. She'd been content enough over the years despite the fact theirs had not been a marriage based on love. Robert had treated her like a pet he doted upon, and she'd done her best not to dwell on what might have been. Andrew had left for Europe just before her marriage had taken place, and she'd been grateful she didn't need to worry about running into him in Town. And when she'd learned of his return a few years later, she'd fled, retiring to spend the majority of her time at Hathaway's estate in Northampton.

Over the years she'd managed to accept her lot in life, but she'd never forgotten him. When her solicitor had asked her if it was possible she was with child, she'd known she wasn't. Robert had been eager to conceive a child with her and had visited her regularly over the years, but had stopped a few short months ago when he fell ill.

That question, though, had sparked a ridiculous idea that wouldn't leave her. Especially when she realized she now had an excuse to approach Andrew and attempt to fill the emptiness that had grown inside her since she'd let her parents convince her to give him up.

She had no illusions that he'd been pining for her all these years, just as she was also under no illusion about her likelihood of falling with child from their time together. She hadn't been able to conceive a child in the twelve years of her marriage, and since Robert already had an illegitimate daughter when they married, she knew the fault lay with her. Her courses had never come regularly, not like they did with other women, and as the years passed she had no other option than to accept the fact she was barren.

But now she had an opportunity—an opportunity she would not so easily throw away as she'd done when she was a foolish girl of eighteen. She would finally learn what it was like to be physically intimate with the man she loved.

She tested the door and, finding it unlocked, let herself in. Two oil lamps lit the hallway, but other than that the house seemed empty. In the unnerving quiet, her heart sounded loud to her own ears. She took an inventory of her surroundings and saw right away the rooms on the main floor were dark, but light beckoned from the second level. Unnerved by the silence and the gloom surrounding her, she made her way upstairs, the light serving as a beacon.

The door to the room at the top of the stairs was ajar, and when she pushed it open, she wasn't surprised to find herself in a bedroom. Most of the furniture was simple but for one notable exception—the bed. It dominated the small space, appearing a good deal larger than any she'd ever seen. The curtains at the windows were closed, the light from the fireplace and an oil lamp on the sole bedside table making the room seem cozy and welcoming. Miranda moved to the fire blazing in the hearth and held out her hands to warm them. It was still early enough in the spring that evenings were much cooler than during the day.

Questions rose, unbidden, about just how many other women Andrew had brought here over the years, but she pushed the unwanted thoughts from her mind. She had no right to begrudge him the companionship of other women. Not after she had denied him her own.

She spun around at the sound of a floorboard creaking behind her and found herself face-to-face with Andrew. He stood several feet away, his features in shadow, which somehow made the effect of his presence more intimate since it highlighted what they were both here to do.

She had a moment of doubt, wondering if the now mature Earl of Sanderson could live up to her memories of the young Andrew Osborne she'd met and fallen in love with twelve years before. He was different, harder, but the years had been good to him. The attractive, charming young man had blossomed into a man of account.

He wore his hair short now. She remembered how, when it was longer, the brown had been threaded through with blond highlights that had given him a tousled, almost boyish appearance. In its current close-cropped style, his hair looked much darker than its medium brown. His face had also lost its youthful appearance, the slight roundness gone. It was more angled than she remembered, his square jaw and cheekbones more prominent.

His eyes, however, were the same. A medium green unlike any she had ever seen before or since. She used to adore gazing into them when they danced at those many balls that one season they'd had together. But now they mocked her. Gone was the warmth she'd once found in their depths.

Her heart was racing… whether from fear or anticipation, she wasn't sure. Probably a little of both. She did her best to keep her breathing even, however. Having made such an outrageous proposition as asking him to help her conceive a child, she could hardly act the part of a shy virgin. At any rate, she was far from being that.

It seemed Andrew planned to just stand there, probably hoping to make her nervous, so she broke the silence. "I find it hard to believe we are both here, about to do this thing."

He raised a brow. "You cannot possibly be more surprised than I."

He bridged the last few steps that separated them, stopping only when their bodies were almost touching. She knew then he wanted to intimidate her. Gain the upper hand. She wouldn't allow her nervousness to show, but she did feel at a disadvantage when she had to tilt her head back to look up at him.

For one horrible moment she feared he expected

her to act first. Relief flooded through her, therefore, when he took her hands in his much larger ones and brought them up, around his neck. He was so much taller than her that in this position her body was flush against his.

Everything else faded away as they stood like that, she pressed against him, their eyes locked and the air of anticipation swirling around them. Gone were the memories of the many unsatisfactory couplings she'd shared with her husband. The panic she'd undergone when he'd died and she realized she was now truly alone in the world, for she would never again go back to her family and allow them to control her life. Even the desperation that had led her to proposition the Earl of Sanderson so she could finally feel, if only for a little while, what it was like to be happy again.

For she was happy just being here with him. She hadn't expected that.

"I'm not going to ask if you're still sure you want to do this," he said.

She had no second thoughts, but his statement surprised her. The Andrew she'd known had always been considerate to a fault.

She spoke around a mouth that had suddenly gone dry. "Why not?"

"Because I don't want to know if you've changed your mind. You made your offer and I accepted. There's no turning back now."

He'd lowered his head and his last words were spoken against her lips. When she opened her mouth to reply—she couldn't say with what—he took it as an invitation to kiss her. This time there was no gradual buildup. The kiss was hot and hungry, and she dove into it without hesitation.

Yes, this was what she wanted. Andrew holding her, kissing her as though he wanted to devour her. His hands moved to her backside and pressed her more firmly against his impressive erection. She realized she was making mewling sounds low in her throat. Perhaps she should have been embarrassed in case he believed her wanton, but she couldn't bring herself to care. With this man only, she *felt* wanton. Deliciously so.

He must have taken her physical response as the answer to the question he hadn't wanted to ask and walked her backward until her legs bumped against the edge of that enormous bed. He moved away from her then, but only a fraction so he could lift her into his arms and deposit her in the center. He joined her there, covering her with the heat of his body, and she shivered with need. This was nothing like the rushed, emotionless couplings she'd shared with her husband.

She expected him to raise her skirts and bury himself inside her, so was confused when he levered himself away to kneel on the bed beside her.

"Is something the matter?" She was shocked at how hoarse her voice sounded to her own ears.

"You're wearing too many clothes."

She didn't protest when he pulled her into a kneeling position before him and removed the cloak she'd only just realized she was still wearing. He made a strangled sound when he saw the red gown she wore with its very low bodice. She'd been uncertain whether to be so brazen when dressing, but now she was glad she'd chosen the provocative dress.

"I promise to take time to appreciate you in that dress later, but for now, it has to go."

He shifted until he was behind her and started to work his way down the row of buttons. Her mind blanked. Surely he didn't mean to actually disrobe her? Never, in all her years of marriage, had Hathaway removed her clothing. Then again, she'd always worn her nightdress when he came to her, so perhaps Andrew would stop when she was down to her chemise.

Her wayward thoughts scattered when he loosened her stays. When the undergarment was held up only by the loosened bodice of her gown, he placed his warm hands on her shoulders and lowered her dress. She moved to take her arms out of the sleeves, but he pulled the garment tight around her again, stilling her movement. She remained that way, her arms trapped, her breathing quickening, while he drew the stays from her body. He pulled her back against him and cupped her breasts through her chemise.

He groaned and the sound echoed deep within her. He completely surrounded her. The coolness of his satin waistcoat chilled her back through her thin chemise while his warm hands squeezed and played with her breasts. Not caring what he might think of her, knowing only that she needed more of what he was doing to her, she let her head fall back against his shoulder and thrust her breasts more firmly into his hands. When he tweaked her nipple between his thumb and forefinger, she moaned. Heat spread from his hands and traveled though her body, moving across her belly and settling lower, between her legs.

She struggled against the constraints of her dress and he relented, moving away and helping her to remove her arms and allowing the dress to fall to the bed around her. She tried to turn and reach for him, but he wouldn't allow it. He untied the tape at the top of her chemise and before she realized his intention, he'd dragged her undergarment down as well. She should have been embarrassed, kneeling on the bed, all her clothes pooled around her, but at that point she was far from caring about her modesty. She craved the touch of his hands on her body again, and the idea of lying bare-skinned with him was more exciting than she could have imagined.

She expected him to touch her breasts again, waited almost breathlessly for it. With a low curse, he moved from the bed and started removing his own clothing. She watched, her attention riveted on his quick, efficient movements as he cast aside his topcoat and waistcoat, untied his cravat, and drew his shirt over his head.

She'd known his chest was broader now—assumed it had happened when he'd shaken off the last of his youthful appearance—but she hadn't realized he was so muscular. He looked back at her then and, catching her staring at him, let out a sound she could only describe as a growl.

He made quick work of his shoes, trousers, and smallclothes, then stood there, fully erect before her, as though waiting for her to comment.

"When you marry one day, your wife will be most fortunate."

At his scowl she realized it was the wrong thing to say, but she didn't have time to examine why. He climbed back onto the bed, and when he eased her onto her back, she went willingly. He slid an arm under her hips, lifting her so he could strip her gown and chemise from where it had tangled against her legs. She could only stare at him, her breathing heavy, as he removed first one slipper, tracing his fingers along the high arch of her foot, then the other. He repeated the caress before smoothing his hands along her calves. When he reached her knees, she feared she'd stop breathing, but he continued until he reached her garters. They were red, like her dress.

"Did you wear these for me?" he asked, stroking the skin above them.

His eyes, when they met hers again, were a dark green, and the emotion she saw reflected there told her he was just as affected as she.

In truth, she hadn't expected him to see the garters, but she nodded in response. He rewarded her with quick kisses, high on each thigh, through her drawers, and she almost jumped out of her skin. He rolled the garters and stockings from her legs and cast the flimsy garments away. His smooth movements told her more than anything else that this was far from the first time he had performed such an intimate action with a woman.

When he started to remove her drawers, panic surged through her. She grabbed his forearms, halting him.

"Must you?"

She'd barely managed the words as she felt the first real twinges of alarm.

"All or nothing, Miranda."

She hesitated only a moment longer before nodding. She squeezed her eyes closed and lifted her hips while he removed the garment, unbearably self-conscious. She knew he was staring at her body, taking in the sight of her hips, which were as slender as a boy's, and her most intimate of places. Not even her husband had seen her completely in the nude.

He eased himself over her, and she moaned at the feel of his hot, hard body, pressing her into the mattress, his erection branding the outside of her thigh. She fought the urge to run her hands all over the smooth expanse of his skin.

"Open your eyes," he said, his voice rough. "When

I take you, I want you to know who you're with."

She could hardly mistake this man for her husband. The two did not even appear to belong to the same species. She opened her eyes and they stayed like that for what seemed a lifetime, his eyes ensnaring hers and their bodies touching from chest to thigh. She wasn't sure who moved first, but their mouths met in a hot, urgent kiss.

She brought her hands up to encircle his neck, her fingers weaving into his short hair and keeping his head right where she wanted it. Her mouth opened wide, allowing him full access. He took advantage, but she didn't remain passive. Her tongue tangled with his and she gave as good as he.

She allowed herself to explore him then, running her hands across his shoulders and down the muscles of his arms. When she snaked her arms around his waist, he made an almost-strangled sound and tore his mouth from hers.

The next time his head dipped, it was lower than she'd expected. He placed his mouth on her neck, trailing warm kisses along its length. The heat of his breath caused an almost unbearable yearning within her. He didn't stop there but moved even lower, nibbling playfully on her shoulder before proceeding to rain kisses down to her breast. He kneaded one breast while he trailed his tongue across the slope of the other. When he took the nipple into his mouth and sucked hard, she arched off the bed. He held her down, continuing to torture her with his mouth and hands as pleasure speared through her.

She needed to have him inside her and opened her legs. The tip of his shaft slid along her wet folds and she moaned.

"Shh. Not yet." The words were softly spoken, but they seemed to echo in the room.

He trailed more kisses down her abdomen, startling her. When he continued his downward path, she tried to close her legs. His hands on her knees easily prevented the movement.

"Andrew, don't…"

She jumped when he slid his hands high up on her thighs and held her there, his thumbs almost touching her opening. "What are you doing?"

He looked up and the naked lust in his eyes stole the rest of her protest.

"You proposed this arrangement—it's all or nothing. I want to do this."

He waited for her assent. She was uncomfortable with him seeing her so intimately, but at that moment she knew she would do anything for him. She also knew that despite what had happened in the past and how he had changed, she trusted him. If she hadn't, she never would have approached him.

She nodded and started to close her eyes but then, remembering what he'd said about giving him everything, kept her gaze on him. She had difficulty holding still when he placed a kiss high on the inside of her thigh. He stared at her there, between her legs, and she fought the urge to turn away from him. With his thumbs he held her open, which confused her. Why would he want to look at her down there?

"I've imagined doing this to you."

Before she could ask what he meant, his mouth covered her intimately and she jerked in shock.

His tongue swept along the place where she knew her center of her pleasure rested. Her husband had never touched her there—she'd had to discover it on her own. Having Andrew between her legs now, his tongue stroking her along that spot, was almost too much to bear. She was wetter than she had ever been, and the heat of his mouth, his tongue... Oh God, he entered her with two fingers and moved them in rhythm with his tongue.

She could no longer bear it. She closed her eyes

and light exploded behind her lids, her hips bowing up off the bed. She might have yelled, but she was too overcome, and too astonished, to be sure.

He covered her in a flash. His manhood pressed against her and she opened her legs wider to welcome him. When he surged inside in a sudden, smooth thrust, she gasped in surprise. Surprise because there was no pain, only pleasure at finally being filled.

"Look at me, Miranda."

And she did. He moved, his thrusts deep and steady at first. She panted but never broke eye contact. This she knew. She'd experienced this thrusting with her husband far too many times over the years. It had never been like this, however. With Hathaway she had only wanted it to be over quickly. But now she wanted it to go on forever.

Instinctively, she wrapped her legs around his lean hips and arched up to meet each of his thrusts. Her breathing quickened. Staring deep into Andrew's eyes, she almost felt as though she could touch his soul. What she saw there scared her a little. Desire, certainly, but also satisfaction. He knew she had never experienced such pleasure with her husband, and he reveled in the knowledge that he was showing her everything she had missed over the years by choosing

Hathaway over him.

She allowed him that satisfaction, for he'd more than earned it. Her entire world centered on Andrew in that moment. All that mattered was him.

She climbed toward that same peak again and could no longer maintain eye contact. She threw her head back and panted each time he drove into her. His pace increased and he pressed his lips against her throat and murmured words she could not understand.

"Now, Miranda," he said, lifting his head again to look down at her.

Unable to resist the command, she came apart in his arms. He continued to move inside her, drawing out the moment of ecstasy until, with a groan, he buried himself deep inside her and joined her with his release.

He collapsed against her and they lay like that for some time. His heavy weight against her comforted her and she wished they could stay like that forever. But even as she tried to draw comfort from his warmth, bone-deep regret began to spread through her. She'd been a fool to let herself be so easily swayed all those years ago. She never should have allowed her parents to convince her to give up Andrew.

CHAPTER THREE

HE NEEDED TO move. To get off her, get dressed, and leave. Instead, he rolled onto his side and drew her to him. She snuggled against him, hiding her face in his chest, and he hated how good it felt.

Miranda had gotten what she'd wanted from him. No, she'd gotten more. He could tell she hadn't expected to orgasm. He shouldn't ask the question— he already knew the answer—but he couldn't help himself. "Was it like that with Hathaway?"

A full minute passed and he didn't think she was going to reply.

"No," she said finally. Simply.

Satisfaction filled him, along with a hint of relief that she hadn't volunteered further details. He'd needed to know that at least in this one thing he'd surpassed her expectations. Lord knew, he hadn't been enough for her in the past. He didn't want to think about her in another man's bed, however, so the less she said, the better for his peace of mind.

They stayed like that for some minutes as their breathing slowed and their bodies cooled. Only when he began to harden again did he push her away. Without speaking, he gathered her clothes and tossed them onto the bed. The sight of her, hair disheveled, face flushed, and lips full, partially open... his eyes moved lower. Her slight body remained on display and he was sorely tempted to tie her to the bed and keep her there for a week.

He had to call on his considerable self-discipline to turn his back and begin dressing. He heard her moving behind him, heard the rustle of fabric, but steeled himself not to turn around.

"Andrew?"

God, he had to get out of here. Now.

"What?" His tone was more abrupt than he'd intended.

"I require assistance."

He took a deep breath and, gathering all his reserve, turned to face her. She stood there in her chemise, her drawers and stockings back in place. He could see her nipples, the dark triangle of hair, and those damn red garters through the thin material of her chemise. His head started to pound and it took him a few moments to realize she was holding up her stays.

"Turn around," he said, the words almost strangling in his throat. She did, holding the corset against her front. He stared at her back, wanting nothing more than to strip the flimsy chemise from her body again and throw her back onto the bed. Somehow he kept himself from cursing aloud as he moved behind her and began lacing the strings of her stays.

"You've done this before."

Did he detect a tremor in her voice? No, probably not. She appeared to be collected while he was a mass of desire and emotion.

Anxious to be away from her, he didn't reply. He gave the garment one last sharp tug, finished tying the knot, and went back to his own dressing.

When he was done, more than ready by then to

put distance between himself and Miranda Hathaway, he turned around. She'd donned her gown, but it gaped open and she was struggling to do up the buttons herself. This time he didn't hold back his curse, and she looked up, startled.

They stared at each other for several long moments before she turned and waited for his assistance, the very picture of patience. A hint of anger slithered though him. How dare she remain so unaffected while he could barely contain himself? Needing to ruffle her calm demeanor, he moved behind her and placed his hands on her waist. She stood almost unnaturally still.

"What are you doing?"

He smiled with satisfaction when he heard the unmistakable quiver in her voice. That was better.

"Nothing. I was just wondering when you wanted to do this again. One time without precautions only suffices when one doesn't wish to be with child."

His hands moved to the row of buttons and she waited until he had finished before turning to him. Her flush had deepened. Knowing she'd never been one to color with embarrassment, he could only surmise it was from desire and his body stirred.

"What do you suggest? I don't want to be an

imposition."

He gave a bark of laughter at that. "Sweet, making love to a beautiful woman is never an imposition."

He froze when he realized he'd used his old endearment for her. If she noticed, though, she gave no indication. When she seemed at a loss as to how to answer, he continued.

"When did you last have your monthly courses? And are they regular?"

She looked away, clearly disconcerted by the question.

"We are both adults here, Miranda. These things are natural, and when one is intimate with another the subject will arise."

She couldn't conceal her surprise. "If you insist. I can tell you that in my experience, the subject was never once raised in my marriage."

He wondered at that. It was clear Miranda's marriage hadn't been a passionate one, but surely there must have been a time when Hathaway wanted his rights as a husband and she'd had to put him off.

"You are evading the question."

She hesitated before replying. "My first day of bleeding was one week ago, the same day my husband died. How is that for a morbid twist of fate? And before you ask, I don't expect it again for at least three and a half weeks."

He didn't show it, but the news sent a surge of anticipation through him. Three weeks, at least. Surely he could slake his lust for Miranda Hathaway in that time and finally consign all thoughts of her and what might have been to the past, once and for all.

"In that case, I suggest we meet daily for the next three weeks." She balked, but he spoke over her protests. "You don't have the luxury of trying for months on end. If you want others to believe the baby you carry belongs to your husband, you need to do everything within your power to conceive this month."

She took a shaky breath and licked her lips before replying, and he held back a groan, hoping she wouldn't look down and notice he was already hard again.

"Very well," she said with a small nod.

"Good. My carriage is waiting for me not too far away. I'll arrange to have another carriage come to the house for you. There's an extra key on the fireplace mantel so you can lock up when you leave." He strode to the door, already anticipating what he would do to her the following evening. "Oh, and Miranda," he said, turning when he'd reached the threshold, "fancy dresses really aren't needed. I won't care what you're wearing since your clothing will be removed as soon as you arrive."

CHAPTER FOUR

MIRANDA TOOK ANDREW at his word and wore
something simple the next night. She chose a sky-blue
day gown to wear under her dark cloak, not having it
in her to wear mourning colors. Despite the fact that
she hadn't been in love with Robert and the fact that
theirs had not been a passionate marriage, she'd still
cared for him. And he'd always been good to her.

She tried not to think about how disappointed
he'd be with her if he could see what she was doing.
Her actions were the height of selfishness, but she
knew that without the excuse of asking Andrew to

help her sire an heir, she would never have had the courage to approach him for a traditional affair. Worse, she feared he would have laughed in her face. He'd been shocked by her proposal, but she'd counted on him wanting revenge against her husband. She'd hurt Andrew and it was human nature to want to lash back at the person who'd caused that hurt. Some might say she was being naïve, but she trusted that he wouldn't hurt her, but he could strike back at the memory of her husband.

The fact that he'd shown her passion beyond her wildest imaginings was something she hadn't expected. After twelve years of marriage, and the increasingly frantic and frustrated couplings she'd been subjected to by Robert when she failed to fall pregnant month after month, who would have thought she'd be so ignorant about the business of lovemaking?

After arriving home the night before, she'd taken out the slim volume of erotic art she'd found in her husband's bedroom after his death. She hadn't been able to make herself look through it before, but did so then with the hope of learning how to give Andrew the same pleasure he had shown her. She knew he'd been satisfied, she'd felt him finish, but she hated the idea that he might soon become bored with her. It was clear he didn't lack for female companionship, and for the short time they would be together she didn't want him sliding into boredom brought on by her obvious lack of carnal knowledge.

Filled with anticipation for the evening to come, she unlocked the front door and entered the house. Just as it had been the night before, the first floor was in darkness save for the light of the two lamps. She climbed the stairs, the bedroom on the second floor her destination. This time, Andrew was waiting for her in the room. On the bed. He'd already removed his boots and coat, and his relaxed posture made her ache to join him.

At her entrance he looked up from the book he'd been reading, a sensual smile forming on his wicked lips. He closed the book and placed it on the nightstand.

"I've always appreciated the fact that you're never late," he said, leaning back against the headboard. He folded his arms across his chest and watched her.

Feeling self-conscious, she removed her cloak and draped it over a chair. When she turned back to face him, he remained motionless, watching her intently. The way he seemed to devour her with his eyes should have embarrassed her. Before last night, it would have. Now, however, the heat in his eyes only served to heighten her desire.

Since he showed no sign of moving, she raised her hand to undo the dress's hook at the nape of her neck. The movement caused her breasts to thrust forward, and the appreciation in Andrew's eyes spurred her to continue.

She'd made sure to choose a dress that would be easy for her to remove on her own. She lowered her arms and bent them behind her back to undo the second hook in the middle of her back and the one at her waist. That was all it took to loosen the bodice. With a simple movement of her shoulders, it slid down her arms. Andrew lifted a brow in surprise when he realized she wasn't wearing a chemise.

She stepped out of the dress and bent to retrieve it, and her breasts threatened to spill out from the short corset she'd worn. She knew Andrew waited to see if they'd succeed, and when she straightened he let out a sound of disappointment. She placed her dress over her cloak on the chair and stepped out of her shoes before turning back to stand before him in her short corset, stockings, and drawers. This bravado was new to her and her resolve not to show how nervous she felt slipped a notch when Andrew didn't move, his eyes half-lidded with desire, waiting to see what she was going to do next.

When the silence stretched on, she realized he was making a statement. He'd been willing to take the upper hand yesterday, but now he was letting her know if she wanted to make love, she was going to have to take the initiative. Fine. If that was how he wanted the evening to proceed, she was up for the challenge. She straightened her shoulders and approached the bed. Climbing onto it, she kneeled sideways beside him.

His nostrils flared, and from the rigidness of his posture she could tell his restraint was costing him dearly. She held back a smile of satisfaction. His eyes remained fixed on her breasts when she leaned forward to unbutton his waistcoat. He shifted toward her when she reached the last button so she could draw the garment off his shoulders and down his arms. She started to rise from the bed, to bring the garment to the chair, when he clamped a hand around her wrist to stop her.

She froze. Their eyes caught and held, and the very air thickened around them. He released her arm but held her in place, instead, by gripping her waist. His warm hands burned into the bare skin between her corset and drawers, where he stroked her in maddeningly slow circles. Reminding herself to breathe, she laid the waistcoat on the bed beside them and raised her hands to untie the knot in his cravat. She unwound it and tossed the rumpled piece of fabric next to the waistcoat.

She couldn't resist touching the skin that showed above the open neck of his shirt. His flesh was hot, and a few hairs peeked out from beneath the bottom of the opening. His pulse beat an erratic rhythm under her caress.

"You're killing me," he said, his voice tense.

This time she didn't hide her smile. In a swift movement, she tugged his shirt from the waist of his trousers and, with his help, lifted it over his head. She placed her hands over his chest and elicited a sharp intake of breath from him when she ran her hands over its broad expanse. Gathering the rest of her nerve, she lowered her hands and traced the muscles of his abdomen before following the line of hair down to where it disappeared into his trousers. She'd never performed such an intimate act for her husband, so her hands weren't steady when she reached for the fall of his trousers and undid the buttons. She could feel his erection straining against the barrier and a shiver of anticipation raced through her.

Tension fairly vibrated from Andrew and she knew he warred between allowing her to continue and taking control. When she pulled the fall aside and reached in to stroke the hard length of his arousal through his smallclothes, he lost the battle. Before she realized what was happening, he'd reversed their positions and pushed her down onto the bed amid the pile of his clothing.

"Your clothes…"

"I could not possibly care less about whether my waistcoat will be wrinkled," he said through gritted teeth. To underscore his words, he shifted her aside to grab the offending articles of clothing and tossed them onto the floor.

Miranda remembered how much Hathaway had hated to be seen less than impeccably dressed. The fact that Andrew did not share the same concern— that he seemed only to care about being with her— sent another thrill of excitement through her.

He quickly stood to remove his last remaining garments and joined her, again, on the bed. This time, however, he straddled her. In this position she couldn't ignore his erection, which jutted out proudly from its thatch of dark hair. Venturing into territory about which she knew nothing, but anxious to learn more, she reached out to touch him.

"Like this," he said, taking her hand and wrapping it around his erection and showing her how to slide her hand up and down. She marveled at the softness of his skin that covered his hard length.

Remembering one of the drawings she had seen in her husband's book, she gave his shaft one final squeeze before releasing him.

"I would like to try something," she said, her voice husky with arousal. "If you would…"

She placed her hands on his thighs and pushed. She wouldn't have been able to move him if curiosity hadn't gotten the better of him. He hesitated only a moment before moving off her. He kneeled at her side as she rose to a sitting position.

"On your back."

He raised a brow at her command but complied. He lay, sprawled on the bed, every masculine inch of him on display. She drank in the sight. The perfection of his body almost overwhelmed her and she couldn't help but wonder how many other women had seen him this way over the years. For that matter, she didn't even know if he currently had a mistress.

The jealousy that swept over her was overwhelming and decidedly unwelcome. Andrew wasn't married and he'd never said she would be his only lover. She hated the idea that he might be sharing these same intimacies with another woman but tried to push aside the images that rose in her mind at the thought. She needed to concentrate on the present and the moments she could steal with Andrew Osborne.

Remembering the way he had touched her the night before and the heightened pleasure it had aroused, she leaned over him and explored his body with her hands and mouth. When she flicked her tongue over his nipple, he jerked.

"If you're going somewhere with this, you'd better hurry. I won't be able to restrain myself much longer." His voice was rough and she knew it was testing the very limits of his self-control to hold back. Even at the young age of nineteen, he'd been a man of action—rarely content to sit and wait, and certainly not one to let others take the lead.

She ran a trail of hot, openmouthed kisses down his abdomen. When she reached his manhood, every muscle in his body was taut.

"Miranda…" His voice held a hint of warning.

Not sure what she was doing, relying only on that

drawing she had seen, she wrapped her right hand around the base of his erection and took him into her mouth. He almost jumped off the bed and the groan that escaped him filled the room.

Remembering how he'd wanted her to stroke him with her hand, she began to move her mouth up and down on him. He tangled his hands in her hair, helping her with the rhythm. She'd imagined this act would be distasteful and had wanted only to show him the same pleasure he had shown her the night before when he had used his mouth on her intimately. But having him fill her mouth now, the taste and smell of him overwhelming her senses, excited her and she felt a rush of wetness between her thighs. His obvious enthusiasm for her ministrations let her know that he, too, enjoyed what she was doing. She was surprised, therefore, when his hands tightened around her head and he pulled her away from him.

Worried she'd done something wrong, she stared at him for a moment before saying, "I thought you were enjoying it."

"I was—too much—but you won't conceive a child if I spill inside your mouth."

Flustered, she looked away. For those few short moments, she'd actually forgotten they weren't really lovers. She'd had to lie to him so they could have this brief liaison. She might have gotten carried away, but it was clear he hadn't.

She remained kneeling beside him while he rose onto his elbows.

"Take off your drawers," he said.

She'd been so engrossed in what she was doing she'd forgotten she still wore her undergarments, and it was clear Andrew liked to make love without any barriers between them.

She moved to the side of the bed and removed her drawers. She still had on her corset and stockings, but when she started to remove her garters, he told her to stop. Confused, she glanced at him over her shoulder.

"Leave them on and come here."

She hesitated. Somehow, wearing only stockings and a corset, bare in between and the latter pushing her breasts up so they almost spilled over the top, made her feel more exposed than she had yesterday when he'd stripped her of all her clothing.

"Come over here," he repeated.

Doing her best not to show her unease, she moved back onto the bed and sat beside him. It was more than a little ridiculous, given everything that had already happened between them, but she covered her mons with her hands. She expected him to laugh at her belated modesty, but instead his expression was tense.

"On my lap," he said, sitting now.

Evidently she was no longer the one in control of this encounter, so she did what he asked. Taking a deep breath, she moved to sit sideways on his lap, very conscious of his jutting arousal. He placed his hands on her hips, surprising her, and moved her so she was on her knees. He brought her down over him, spreading her legs so she was straddling his thighs, his arousal between them.

He kissed her then, for the first time since she'd entered the room. Unlike the kisses they'd shared the evening before, this kiss was softer, like the start of the first one they'd shared just two days before in her town house when he'd come at her invitation. He spread featherlight kisses on her cheeks, the lids of her closed eyes, even her nose. When he reached her mouth again, he kept the kiss light, brushing his lips over hers. Frustrated, she tried to deepen the kiss, but he held her at bay. When he dragged her lower lip between his teeth, she heaved a sigh of frustration and ground herself against his hard erection, now trapped between them.

That spurred him on because he stopped teasing and opened his mouth to allow her entrance. Almost desperate for another taste of him at that point, she took the lead, exploring his mouth as she had his body. He tangled his tongue with hers and the nature of the kiss deepened. Darkened. They were both panting for breath now.

His hands tightened on her backside, urging her on as she writhed against his erection.

He drew back slightly and spoke against her mouth, the words coming out between harsh breaths as she continued to rub herself against him. "Now, Miranda. Take me inside you."

His desperation inflamed her further and she knew what he wanted her to do. She'd also seen an illustration of this in Hathaway's book. She rose up on her knees until the blunt tip of his manhood was pressed against her entrance, where she was almost impossibly wet. Using one hand to hold him in place, she impaled herself on his hard length.

Her breath huffed out on a long moan when he was finally where she needed him most, deep inside her. In this position, he was deeper than before. She swayed against him and lowered her head onto his shoulder, enjoying the way he filled her.

"You're still killing me," he said in a hoarse voice, his hands flexing on her hips.

He lifted her until just the tip of him was inside her, then dragged her back down. She released her breath on a shaky sigh but followed his lead and started to move up and down over him.

When she had found her rhythm, Andrew turned his attention elsewhere. It took little effort for him to scoop her breasts out from the top of her corset, and she arched into his hot hands while continuing to move over his hard length.

He fondled her, squeezing her breasts as he knew she liked and flicking his thumbs over their stiff points before covering one with his mouth and suckling hard. Shafts of liquid heat shot straight through her to where they were joined.

Her movements became quicker, less elegant, as her heart raced and her breaths came out in pants. He reached between them to touch her right where she needed him, and she exploded around him, his name mixed with another moan.

She sagged against him, spent. He simply held her while her heartbeat slowed. It took her a full minute to realize he was still hard. She lifted her head to look at him.

"You didn't finish."

His green eyes were dark with unfulfilled desire.

"No, but I will."

He lifted her again and slammed her down against him. She was too wrung out to help him, and when he realized that he flipped them over so she was now beneath him, his hardness never leaving her. His face showed signs of strain.

"I can't wait, Miranda."

She lifted a hand and cupped his cheek. "Don't."

He closed his eyes for a moment and moved his face deeper into the caress. But he indulged himself only for a moment before starting to move again. Each thrust was hard, desperate, and before long a similar desperation rose within her. Again. She clung to his shoulders and wrapped her legs around him, meeting each slam of his body against hers.

He didn't last long before arching his back and burying himself deeply one last time. With a guttural sound, he exploded. The rush of his hot seed inside her triggered another orgasm, and she had to bury her mouth against his neck to keep from screaming.

CHAPTER FIVE

Miranda had been expecting James Hathaway for days now, ever since her meeting with the solicitor earlier in the week. She'd been the one to initiate that meeting, but the fact that her husband's nephew was now at the town house caused a wave of sadness, almost suffocating in its intensity, to sweep through her. She'd known this day would come but was still unprepared for the final sign that this phase of her life was over. She wouldn't miss the town house and its ever-present reminder of her marriage, however. What she'd miss most was Andrew.

While she would love nothing more than to remain in town and see if they could have more together, she wasn't foolish enough to believe he wanted the same thing. Andrew hadn't said or done anything in the almost three weeks they'd been together to lead her to believe he would have any difficulty moving on after their affair was over. And she had no doubt there were many other women who would willingly step into her place once she was gone.

She gave her head a small shake, as if doing so could somehow dispel her melancholy thoughts. Nothing would come from delaying the inevitable, so she took a deep breath, collected the cloak of reserve around her that she'd managed to perfect over the years, and made her way to the drawing room.

In the twelve years of her marriage, she had never met her husband's heir. Taking in his appearance as she entered the room and he rose, she could see immediately why Robert had been so distraught at the knowledge that this man would be the next viscount. The long row of portraits of the numerous viscounts that was prominently displayed at the Hathaway estate depicted men who were similar in appearance to her husband—fair-haired and fine-boned. James Hathaway, however, did not fit into that mold.

What struck her first was his size. The man standing before her now could never be confused with the other men who had held the Hathaway title. He stood well over six feet in height and his build... Andrew was muscular, but this man was even broader. In fact, he had the appearance more of a brawler than a peer of the realm. The slight curve in his nose, indicating it had been broken at least once, underscored that perception. And his hair, slightly longer than was fashionable, was black as night.

Miranda couldn't miss the wariness in his expression as he rose. Given that he had never been made to feel welcome by his uncle, she could well understand his reticence.

After a rather awkward greeting, she offered to ring for tea, but he refused. She took a seat on the settee and watched while her nephew lowered himself onto the chair opposite her. As they often did when she was in the drawing room, her thoughts went immediately to Andrew and the first kiss they had shared on that very settee, and she had to force herself to concentrate on the present.

"I am so glad you accepted my invitation," she said, meaning it. She'd always hated the distance that her husband had placed between them and his younger brother's family.

She could almost see the tension easing from the man's body when he realized she wouldn't be treating him with the same disdain her husband has shown him.

"I must admit I was more than a little surprised to receive the letter from your solicitor. After a lifetime of assurances that I would never inherit the title, I find it impossible to believe I am sitting here with you."

He was referring, of course, to her inability to conceive an heir and the fact she was not carrying a child now.

Hoping to reassure him that she bore him no ill will, she gave a small shrug. "Sometimes these things answer to a higher authority."

Her reply seemed to surprise him. He leaned back and examined her closely for several moments before saying, "May I be candid with you?"

"By all means," Miranda said. "Despite what Robert may have chosen to believe, we are family."

A brief flicker of emotion crossed his face at the mention of his uncle, but when he spoke, Miranda was relieved that he clearly didn't wish to address the acrimony between the two families.

"You are not at all what I expected."

She tilted her head to one side, amused at his obvious confusion. "You thought I would be throwing a fit right now? Or that I would be pleading with you for a larger settlement?"

"Frankly, yes. I've seen the terms of the will and your marriage contract. My uncle was less than generous in the eventuality that you did not give birth to the next viscount."

She shrugged. "One cannot predict these things. My parents were very happy with the marriage settlement, and one always assumes that in time children will come."

He hesitated before saying, "It's no secret that the Hathaway estate is a very prosperous one. You should know that I intend to increase the amount of your allowance."

"No!" Guilt had caused her to speak more loudly than she'd intended, and from the expression on James's face she could see he was taken aback by the vehemence of her response. But she could not entertain the idea of seeking a larger income from the Hathaway estate, not after the way her actions were dishonoring her husband's memory even now.

"I would argue that after twelve years of marriage,

it is no less than your due."

"Perhaps," she said, careful to keep further emotion from her voice. "But I am content to live modestly. I have learned over the years that having money does not always mean one will be happy."

The pity on James Hathaway's face told her that she had said too much, and another wave of guilt at tarnishing Robert's memory swept through her. She knew better than to argue that her marriage had not been as bad as he might be thinking. There was no love lost between James and his uncle and he was unlikely to want to hear her defense of him.

"So it is all settled," she continued. "I only ask that you grant me a few days to make preparations to retire to the country."

She knew he would assume that she would move to the dowager house on the Hathaway estate, but chose not to correct that assumption since it served her own plans.

"I want you to know it is not my intention to force you from town. I realize that you cannot socialize until you are out of mourning, but you are welcome to remain here. Or if you'd like, I can help you find a new house."

Miranda realized she liked James Hathaway and

was glad she had finally gotten a chance to meet him, but there was no way she could remain in London after her affair with Andrew ended.

She stood and he rose to his feet as well.

"I thank you for your generosity, but I would prefer the quiet of the countryside right now. I am not removing from town because of you."

He gave her a small nod of acknowledgment. "Very well. I will leave my address with your butler. And if there is anything you need, please know I am at your service."

She remained standing as he left, but her legs gave out as soon as she heard the front door close. Pain lanced through her as she realized it was almost over. Within days she would leave the Hathaway town house and London, and she would never see Andrew again.

CHAPTER SIX

HE WAS LATE, caught up in a particularly heated debate in the House of Lords. As the hours ticked by into the evening, he grew increasingly more bad-tempered. At several points it occurred to him that he should arrange to have his driver deliver a note to Miranda before she left for the house he'd rented, but he couldn't bring himself to cancel the evening. Not while there remained a glimmer of a chance one side might cool down enough for the matter to be resolved.

When it became clear that wouldn't happen, he

could have arranged to have a note delivered to her at the house, but still he held off and that annoyed him more than anything else. He needed to see Miranda. Craved her with a desperation that alarmed him, and with that realization his mood darkened even further.

As the hours passed, curious glances were cast his way as those around him began to sense his dangerous mood. No one approached him until Viscount Morrison was foolish enough to intercept him when the session had finally ended for the night.

"I don't suppose we'll see you at Brooks tonight," the man said with a knowing smirk.

Andrew barely resisted the urge to wipe the smile from the man's face and started to turn away, but Morrison's next words halted him in his tracks.

"There have been a few wagers placed as to the identity of the woman who has captured your interest to the exclusion of all else. I'll admit to more than a small curiosity myself. I don't suppose you'd care to enlighten me?"

The look he aimed at the slight man would have been enough to keep another from continuing. Morrision, however, had never been known to possess much good sense.

"She must be very good. Perhaps I can give her a

go."

Peripherally he became aware that their conversation was drawing the attention of others, but Andrew's attention remained focused on the man before him. Every muscle in his body had tensed at Morrison's last statement, but somehow he managed to keep from planting his fist into Morrison's thin face.

"I don't share." Andrew's words were clipped, his anger barely contained at that point, but the fool continued.

"Oh no, neither do I. I meant when you tire of her, of course."

Morrison paled when Andrew took a step closer and allowed his hands to curl into fists at his side. One more word along the same vein would have been enough to destroy the little control still within his grasp.

Morrison opened his mouth but must have thought better of it, because he closed it again right away. With a quick nod, he turned and fled. Andrew's gaze swung to the group of men that had stood by, watching the scene as it took place. They, too, wisely chose to turn away and pretend nothing had happened.

Without another word to anyone else, Andrew made his way from Westminster and headed straight for the house. It was already nine and he expected Miranda had long since returned home, no doubt thinking he had tired of her and was seeking other pursuits for the night. His pride had balked at the notion of showing any weakness, but now he regretted he hadn't sent her a note telling her he would be late and asking her to wait for him. He didn't want to analyze the part of him that feared she would have received the note and decided to go home anyway.

He didn't realize his heart was racing until he found her in the bedroom. She had fallen asleep waiting for him, and as he took in her slender figure lying beneath the covers, it hit him like a fist to the gut that he still loved her. And they had only three more days until her monthly courses were due. After that, whether or not they had been successful, their affair would be over. It should have been over already, but neither of them had wanted to say the words that would end it, so they waited for nature to end it for them.

His need for her was a bone-deep ache. Refusing to acknowledge the unwelcome emotions going through him, he undressed and slid into bed bedside her. She woke when he drew her into his arms and the sleepy smile on her face made his heart turn over. Damn. It appeared he wasn't going to remain unscathed when his relationship with Miranda ended—again.

He'd been insatiable, making love to her several times. The last time he'd been particularly forceful, and she sighed, remembering the things he had done. Her body ached, but she relished the sensation. Relished lying beside him now as he slept.

Andrew had always taken great pains to make sure she knew his interest in her was merely physical, so he must have been exhausted to allow himself to fall asleep. And she, desperate to know whatever modicum of closeness he chose to share, even if it was only physical, was content to accept their alliance for what it was. Now, watching him as he slept, she felt she'd been given a gift she'd never expected to receive.

His features were softer, making him look younger than his one and thirty years. In some ways, watching him sleep was more intimate than making love to him and her heart yearned for the closeness they had once shared.

She cursed herself for being a fool twice over. First

for having denied her feelings for him all those years ago and allowing her parents to sway her into accepting Hathaway's marriage proposal. But her second, and greater, mistake was the foolishness of her scheme to find a way to be close to him now.

She'd known almost from the start that their physical relationship was full of risks not just to her reputation, but also to her peace of mind. She'd never stopped loving Andrew, but at that moment she couldn't hold back her regret as bitterness threatened to engulf her. A large part of her wished she had never started out to learn what it was like to make love to Andrew Osborne. Now, along with the memories she'd hoped to cling to during the coming years, she'd also have to live with the knowledge of what she could have had if she'd stood firm against her parents' wishes. If she had, he would have asked her to marry him and they would still be together. She'd always known that to be true, but the full import of what she had lost had never been more clear to her.

Panic, remorse, regret… all swam within her and threatened to consume her. Stifling a sob, she rose from the bed and dressed with shaking hands. She allowed herself one more quick glance at the bed.

"Good-bye, Andrew," she whispered before

turning and escaping from the stifling confines of that unassuming house. She'd made her plans well and had no need to return to the Hathaway town house. She would simply disappear.

CHAPTER SEVEN

WHEN ANDREW WOKE the next morning and found himself alone in bed, disgust swept through him. Disgust that he had let down his guard and allowed himself to enjoy the comfort of holding Miranda as he fell asleep, for enjoy it he had. He'd clung to her the night before like a drowning man clinging to a lifeline.

Hoping to fix the damage he'd caused by spending the night, he dressed and went in search of Miranda so he could take his leave. He expected to find her in another room, perhaps the kitchen, but the annoyance he felt at his unwelcome sentimentality the night before changed to disbelief when he realized she wasn't in the house. She hadn't even left a note. A dark sense of foreboding settled over him like a shroud as he made his way from the house.

Not caring who took note of his visit, he called on her later that afternoon. The very last thing he'd expected to learn was that Hathaway's heir had taken up residence.

Andrew was shown to the library and was taken aback by the tall, dark-haired man who joined him a few minutes later. The new Viscount Hathaway bore no resemblance whatsoever to the old one.

After making their introductions, they settled into armchairs across from one another.

Hathaway spoke first. "To what do I owe this honor?"

Andrew was careful to keep his expression neutral. "I heard you were in town and wanted to pay my respects regarding your uncle's passing."

Hathaway leaned back in his chair and gave a short, disbelieving shake of his head. "It will never cease to amaze me how quickly gossip spreads in a place as large as London. I only took up residence this morning." He frowned before continuing. "But why, then, did you ask for my aunt?"

Andrew wondered if Hathaway had learned of his previous visit and decided it would be best to acknowledge that meeting in case he had.

"I've already expressed my condolences to Lady Hathaway, but I wanted to see how she was faring. Hers was, after all, the greater loss."

Hathaway was silent for a moment, as though considering his next words carefully. "I wasn't aware that you and my uncle were friends."

Andrew shrugged. "We weren't. We saw each other often in the Chamber, but usually from opposing sides of far too many bills."

"Ah, so that's why you're here. You want to sound me out on my political leanings."

Andrew grasped at the excuse. "You can hardly blame me for wondering. We had a horrible evening yesterday, and it never hurts to have an additional vote on your side."

Hathaway seemed to accept the excuse. "To be honest, I haven't given it much thought. I do have my personal leanings, of course, but..." He shrugged. "Uncle hated the fact I was his heir, and the few times we saw one another, we never discussed politics. In fact, the few discussions we had centered on how he was going to make sure I didn't inherit. Perhaps if he'd chosen another bride he would have succeeded, but he chose one who couldn't give him what he wanted most."

Considering what Miranda had told him about how her husband had stopped visiting her bed early in their marriage, he found the younger Hathaway's assertions difficult to believe.

"When does the title go to you? I know it's customary to wait to make sure the widow isn't with child."

"She isn't," he said with a wave of his hand. "Lady Hathaway told the family solicitor that my uncle wasn't up to the task for several months, if you catch my meaning."

Andrew's head began to swim with the realization that Miranda hadn't told him the truth. She'd told him her husband hadn't bedded her in years. And was she really barren, or did the fault lie with the elder Hathaway? He knew sometimes it was the man who was at fault and not the woman. Was she so desperate to hold on to her current wealth that she didn't care if everyone knew that any child she might be carrying wasn't fathered by her husband?

He didn't know what to think anymore. He did,

however, know that he had to see Miranda and ask her himself, but he couldn't insist on seeing her right now.

"Yes, well, I'm sorry to have met you under such circumstances." He said the words despite the fact that it was clear James Hathaway was far from mourning. He stood before continuing. "If you would let your aunt know I called and asked after her well-being, I would be grateful." He turned and started to leave, letting Hathaway know that the call was over.

Hathaway followed him to the door. "She's no longer here."

Andrew stopped and turned to face him, anger rising swift and hot. He didn't bother to conceal it. "Tell me you didn't cast her out. That she has somewhere to go."

Hathaway's jaw tightened. When he replied, his words were clipped. "She chose to leave. Her maid, whom she didn't take with her, informed me that she'd had her personal belongings moved out, one trunk at a time, over the past week. I was surprised to learn she'd left behind all her jewelry—even the pieces my uncle had purchased for her."

Dread settled deep in his belly. Andrew needed to speak to Hathaway's servants, to find out what exactly had happened, but he couldn't make such a request without revealing his more-than-casual interest in the new Viscount's aunt.

"I suppose she wanted the comfort of her home on the estate until she can make other arrangements for herself."

"She's a damned strange woman, if you must know, Sanderson. She left a note saying she wasn't returning to the estate or to her parents' home. I've questioned the servants and no one knows where she's gone." He ran his hand through his hair. "What a disaster. Everyone will say I had her cast out into the streets without a penny to her name."

The blood had frozen in Andrew's veins. Miranda had left and no one knew where she was. He wanted to curse, to rail against her foolishness, but somehow he managed to hold himself together and keep from revealing himself.

"It is clear from your worry that is not the case. No doubt she was too deeply affected by her husband's death to think clearly. I'm sure she just needed some time alone and will send word shortly."

"I hope so," Hathaway said.

Andrew made his way from the house. His thoughts kept coming back to one seemingly unalterable fact—Miranda had lied to him. Her husband had never given up trying to beget an heir. He tried not to think about what it must have been like for her to suffer his attentions over the last twelve years. She'd been surprised that first time he'd brought her to fulfillment and he knew she'd never before reached that peak.

He suspected now that she'd never intended to pass off a child of his as the heir to the Hathaway title and fortunes since it appeared everyone involved already knew it wasn't possible that she was with child. And she certainly wouldn't have disappeared if she'd hoped to blatantly pass off a bastard as the heir.

It had all been a lie.

CHAPTER EIGHT

It took Andrew almost one month to find Miranda after she disappeared that last night they were together, much longer than he'd expected. He'd hired Bow Street's finest to investigate, but she had covered her tracks well. Finally, when he started to fear they might never find her, one of the agents learned she'd traveled to a small village in Yorkshire where she was renting a small cottage.

The man who'd discovered her whereabouts assured Andrew that when he'd seen her in the village she'd looked well. That should have been the end of it. When he'd hired the Runners, he'd reasoned that he only wanted to make sure no harm had befallen her, but deep down he'd known he was only lying to himself. Their three weeks together should have been more than long enough to get her out of his system, but somehow she'd managed to burrow deeper under his skin. Damn him for a fool, but he was still in love with Miranda Hathaway.

Now that he knew where she was hiding, he had to see her again. Aside from his unwelcome feelings for her, there were too many questions to which he needed answers.

It took him two more days to reach her. When he finally arrived at the village where she'd last been seen, it was almost evening, and he stopped at the posting inn to leave his horse and ask for directions. He was hot and dirty, and politeness dictated that he rent a room and bathe first before calling on Miranda. He was too close, though. A small, irrational part of him feared that if he delayed further, she might slip away yet again and he would lose his opportunity to see her.

By the time he reached the small cottage twenty minutes later, the sun had almost set. As he stood before the modest home, he couldn't deny the irony that it was, in appearance, very similar to the house he'd rented so he and Miranda could meet in private.

He rapped on the door and didn't have to wait long before a stout woman he assumed to be the housekeeper answered.

"I am here to see Lady Hathaway."

The woman was clearly surprised that a gentleman, alone, would be paying a call on her mistress, but she didn't comment as she showed him into a small sitting room. Miranda sat by the fire, working on a small square of needlepoint, and he took a moment to drink in the sight of her. He enjoyed the way the golden light of the fire gilded her skin and reflected the chestnut highlights in her dark brown hair.

"Who was it, Mrs. Evers?" She looked up then and paled when she saw him standing in the doorway. "I see. Thank you, Mrs. Evers," she said in what was clearly meant as a dismissal.

Andrew didn't miss the way the older woman glanced between the two of them, a speculative gleam in her eye, before inclining her head and turning to leave.

Miranda placed her needlework on a small table and stood. She smoothed her hands over her black skirts in a nervous gesture, and he was alarmed to see she'd grown even thinner over the last few weeks. Seeing the wariness in her expression, he held back the almost overwhelming need to start demanding answers.

"Good evening, Miranda."

She licked her lips before replying, and his groin tightened in response.

"Andrew," she said, allowing him the briefest of curtseys. "I'm surprised to see you here."

"I can imagine," he said, unable to keep the note of bitterness from his voice.

She sat again. "Are you hungry? It is late, but I can ring for tea and refreshments."

He lowered himself into the chair opposite her. "I see we're back to social conventions."

She looked away without replying.

"I thought," he continued, "that after everything we'd shared, we could have parted on better terms. A farewell, perhaps, or a small wave as you ran away from me again."

She raised her shoulders in a small shrug, but he could tell from how stiffly she held herself that the casual movement was far from indicative of how she truly felt. His presence here had rattled her.

"I didn't see the point," she said, meeting his gaze.

"You were tired and needed to sleep. And when I returned home I discovered my courses had arrived. Since I'd failed to conceive a child, I saw no point in remaining."

"Tell me, Miranda. When did James Hathaway move into the house?"

Her lips tightened before she said, "If you're implying that there was anything untoward between us—"

He cut her off with a wave of his hand. "Don't be ridiculous. Even if he was tempted, Hathaway's heir would hardly be foolish enough to do anything to risk the line of succession at this point. He certainly wouldn't want you to fall pregnant."

Her breath blew out in an offended hiss and he didn't know what he'd said wrong.

"Meaning it was James's ambition that kept him from accepting my wanton advances?"

"No, of course not. You are hardly that type of woman."

She was silent for a moment before replying. "I was with you."

How well he remembered. "I find it most curious your husband didn't try harder to produce an heir."

It took her a moment to adjust to the abrupt

change in subject. "I think he took comfort in the knowledge that James was such a capable young man."

She held herself almost unnaturally still when she replied, just as she had when he'd first seen her again in her drawing room almost two months before. He'd been watching her closely and it didn't escape his notice that she couldn't meet his eyes when she spoke the lie. How had he not noticed that telltale giveaway during his first visit when she'd laid out her ridiculous proposal? He'd been so astonished by her suggestion that he hadn't been paying attention to the signs that revealed what was now obvious to him—Miranda was lying.

"That may be true, but a man still wants to have his own son inherit. Nephews and such are never a first choice."

She met his eyes then and he couldn't tell at first what he was seeing in her expression. Defeat? His conscience pricked at him. He'd have preferred her anger. But damn it, he wasn't the one who'd lied.

"It is late and I am tired. I don't have the energy to play these games with you."

He suspected she'd lied, as well, about having received her monthly courses that last night they were together, but he didn't think she was with child. Not after all those years of trying if Hathaway's nephew was to be believed. Despite that knowledge, his eyes moved down to her midsection. She noticed and stiffened.

"What is it you want to hear, Andrew?"

"The truth would be a pleasant change."

She glanced away and considered her response for several seconds before finally saying, "I was wrong to leave without a word to you. I felt awkward after everything we'd done together. I knew we'd failed, and I was a little ashamed at my attempt at deception."

"Liar."

The accusation was softly spoken, but echoed in the room.

"Excuse me?" she managed when she overcame her surprise.

"I'm tired of your lies, Miranda. Tell me, truthfully, why did you leave?"

"I told you everything. I'm sorry if it's not what you want to hear—"

"Do you want to know what I think?" The room was small, their chairs placed close together, and when he leaned forward Miranda had to lean back to maintain the distance between them.

"No" she said, but the words, again, were obviously a lie.

"I think you ran away because you were overwhelmed. I think you knew from the beginning that you couldn't have children, but you latched on to this mad scheme as an excuse to lure me into your bed."

She laughed, the sound brittle. "You have a very high opinion of yourself."

But he'd seen her shock before she'd attempted to conceal it behind false levity.

"I know it's the truth."

"It's clear to me that you wouldn't recognize the truth if it walked right up to you and introduced itself."

"Enough, Miranda." His voice was louder than he'd intended and a stab of guilt went through him when he saw her flinch. He continued in a softer tone. "I spoke to James Hathaway. According to him, his uncle was quite desperate up until the end to ensure he never inherited. A man in that situation would never leave his wife alone year after year. No, a man who wanted to secure his succession would keep trying. I know you lied about that."

She couldn't meet his eyes and silence stretched between them for what seemed an eternity before she finally looked at him.

"You are correct. My husband wasn't at all happy when I failed to fall pregnant each month." She must have seen the anger that surged through him at her admission, because she hastened to add, "He didn't treat me badly, but he was very disappointed in me."

He didn't want to hear the details. Twelve years, and in all that time she'd never known pleasure in the bedroom until she started her affair with him.

"Would you care to know what else I believe to be true?"

She lifted her shoulders in a shrug that was meant to seem indifferent. He could tell she'd guessed he knew everything, but she wasn't about to betray herself.

"I think you still care for me. Why else would you go to such lengths and concoct such a lie to be with me?" He was bluffing, but a man could hope, and hope was all he had to go on at the moment. "But what I don't know is why you ran away."

She laughed at that, a small, self-deprecating sound. "I propositioned you one week after my husband's death and betrayed his memory in the worst possible manner. Do you honestly believe I could go on pretending to be the respectable Dowager Viscountess?"

Now it was his turn to tread carefully. Miranda was as tense as a doe he'd once stumbled upon in a field, and he didn't want to frighten her away by being too aggressive.

"I never would have called at your town house if you hadn't left without a word. Never would have had a reason to question James Hathaway and learn that you'd lied."

She shook her head. "I couldn't."

He reached out and took her right hand in his. She tried to draw it back, but he wouldn't let go.

"Why not?"

He didn't think she was going to reply, but when she did she met his gaze straight on.

"Because you are right. I still care for you, but I know you no longer feel that way about me."

"Miranda—"

"Yes, you agreed to bed me, but I know I was no different to you than the other women you've been with."

"Do you really believe that?"

She swallowed visibly and nodded. "I don't blame

you. I know I hurt you when I accepted Hathaway's suit. I could try to lay the blame on my parents, tell you they were relentless in pressing me to agree. Which is true, but it doesn't change the fact that I was weak. Too worried about disappointing them. So, instead, I disappointed you. I have no excuses, nor do I deserve your forgiveness."

In the face of her misery, he kept his growing good cheer in check. "You're right," he said softly.

She merely nodded again, but her eyes appeared over-bright.

"We seem to have a problem, then," he continued.

"A problem?"

"Yes. In the beginning, I told myself I could do what you asked. Get you with child, then leave, all the while congratulating myself on having bested Hathaway in the end. And I could finally satisfy my curiosity about what it would be like to have you under me, screaming out my name."

She looked away, saying nothing.

"It did not take me long to realize I was wrong. I could never have left you to raise our child alone, let alone allow you to pass him off as another man's son."

She swallowed. "Yes, well, you needn't worry about any of that now."

"Perhaps not, but what about my discovery that I can't let you go a second time?"

When her eyes met his again, they were wide with disbelief. "What are you saying?"

He clasped her hand between both of his and prepared to bare his soul. "I love you, Miranda. I've always loved you and I know now that will never change. I want you for my own."

"As your mistress?" The words were barely above a whisper.

"No, Miranda, as my wife."

Her choked sob was not the reaction he'd expected. He'd hoped to see joy at his declaration, but instead a tear escaped and trailed down her cheek. She brushed it away with her free hand and he noticed that it shook. His heart squeezed painfully as she tried to pull away again, but he wouldn't release his grip on her hand.

"You deserve to marry someone who can give you children."

"We still don't know that you can't."

"Robert has a daughter," she said, her voice flat. "She was born to a mistress years before he married me, so the fault for my never falling pregnant did not lie with him."

He'd already come to terms with the possibility he would never have children before he'd set out after Miranda. But now he had to make her believe that.

"These last few weeks without you have shown me that I cannot bear to live without you. I barely survived the first time. Don't ask me to go through that again."

"You'll come to resent me. After all, a man still wants to have his own son inherit. Nephews and such are never a first choice."

Her mimicry of the words he'd used when he was trying to draw the truth from her sent a surge of anger through him.

"I'm not Hathaway, damn it, so don't tar me with the same brush. Do I want you to have my children? I won't lie and say no." This time he allowed her to pull her hand away, but he followed and kneeled before her, grasping her thighs in a vain effort to keep her anchored, because he was suddenly afraid she would disappear from his life again. "Unlike your husband, I love my sisters and their many children. Given a choice between Jane's eldest inheriting and marrying some other woman just to procure an heir…" His grip tightened. "I'd much rather have you."

She closed her eyes and a spasm of pain crossed her face.

He didn't bother to hide his hurt when he continued. "Why is it so easy for you to cast me aside?"

She opened her eyes and looked down at him. "You think this is easy for me? I've barely eaten or slept since I left you. I could think of nothing else but how much I wanted to go back and beg you to allow me some small part of your life. But marriage..." She shook her head. "I can't do that to you. You deserve better."

"What I deserve is the woman I love."

She started to reply but instead burst into sobs. Horrified, he pulled her from her chair until she kneeled on the floor with him and drew her into his arms. He was afraid she'd resist, but instead she clung to him until her tears began to slow.

"I am so ridiculous," she said, the words muffled against his shoulder.

He pulled back so he could see her face. "I refuse to allow you to insult the woman I love."

The smile she gave him was tremulous, but it made his heart lighten.

"What am I going to do with you?"

He raised a brow and gave her an exaggerated leer. "I can think of a thing or two."

She laughed—a genuine sound of joy this time—and he'd never heard anything so wonderful in his life.

"I'm still in mourning and will be for the next ten months."

"I can wait if I know you'll marry me at the end of it."

"Then I suppose we're waiting."

He gave a whoop of joy and sprang to his feet, drawing her up with him so he could swing her around. She gave a small squeak of surprise and wrapped her arms around his neck.

"But I refuse to wait a moment longer before making love to you again."

This time when she smiled her tears were gone, as was her uncertainty.

"Then you should put me down so I can tell Mrs. Evers she can go home now."

His eyes followed her as she left the room to find her housekeeper. It would be hard to wait until he could claim her as his own, but he'd do it. Miranda was worth it.

EPILOGUE

THEY WAITED ONLY eleven more months to announce their engagement—one month after Miranda's period of mourning had officially ended. Miranda returned to town after Andrew found her and they were careful to keep their relationship a secret from everyone until she was out of mourning. Shortly after the announcement was made, they were married in a private ceremony with only their family as witnesses at the chapel on Andrew's estate.

"I'm worried about James," Miranda said.

The wedding breakfast had ended a short time

before, and she and Andrew had left their guests to escape to the bedroom.

"Perhaps we can talk about your nephew another time," Andrew said, frowning down at her.

She ignored him and continued. "He's so aloof around Sarah. I don't think he's happy."

Andrew snorted. "Hathaway adores his wife."

He tried to draw her to the bed, but she held her ground.

"How can you say that? The two of them barely looked at one another during breakfast."

"Only a man in love can see the signs in another. He was trying too hard to make it appear as though he was barely aware of her presence. A man does that when he cares too much and doesn't believe his affections are returned."

Miranda frowned. "Is that what you did?"

"Of course. After being tossed aside once by you, I wasn't going to let you know how much you still affected me."

She allowed him to turn her around and begin undoing the row of buttons down the back of her wedding dress while she went over the meal they'd just shared in her mind.

"Why do you think he doesn't want her to know

he cares about her?"

"I can't imagine. Perhaps the fact that she can barely bring herself to even look at him?"

Miranda had noticed that as well. "It could be she's shy. I've known a few women who were that quiet, and yes, even with their husbands."

Andrew laughed. "The new Lady Hathaway is not shy."

He'd finished the buttons and was working now on untying her corset.

"How do you know that?"

"Because I've been to a few social events when her parents were trying to marry her off. She could flirt with the best of them."

He drew her dress down her arms and removed her corset and she turned to face him again. His eyes were hungry as he took in her shape beneath the near-transparent chemise. Her blood heated in response, but she held him back with a hand to his chest.

"Do you think her parents forced the marriage?"

He shrugged. "They would hardly be the first set of parents to set their cap for the Hathaway fortunes."

Miranda frowned at the reminder that her parents had done just that. "But if she cares for him and he cares for her, why would they need to be so formal with one another?"

Andrew exhaled, the sound impatient. "I think your romantic imagination is running away from you. I saw no indication that she cares for him."

"She does. You didn't see the look in her eyes when we were talking about him earlier."

"I'll have to take your word for it. But perhaps it wouldn't be remiss if she showed him she cared."

"The way he shows her?" She laughed and sat on the edge of the bed. "Oh, what a pair. I wonder if we should make them aware of their feelings since they seem to be so oblivious."

Andrew lowered himself onto the bed beside her. "In cases like this, it's best to come to such a realization on your own. I would have flattened anyone who'd so much as hinted that I was still in love with you, and I have no wish to be on the receiving end of your nephew's fists."

"I could talk to him—"

"Absolutely not," he said, lowering her onto the bed and shifting so he was atop her. "They need to figure this out for themselves. We could both be mistaken."

She was finding it difficult to concentrate on the subject, but was about to insist when he placed a finger over her lips.

"Promise me, Miranda. Meddling will only make it worse."

She drew his finger into her mouth and watched as his eyes darkened before releasing it.

"Just a small nudge?"

Andrew didn't bother to hide his impatience to be done with the conversation. "They are already married and there is nothing more we can do."

"You're right, of course," she said, remembering the look of misery on Sarah's face during the wedding breakfast.

That was her last coherent thought before Andrew made her forget everything else but him.

THANK YOU!

Thank you for reading *Lady Hathaway's Indecent Proposal.* If you enjoyed this book, please consider sharing it with a friend. All honest reviews are welcome and appreciated.

If you'd like to learn about future books, you can join my new release newsletter at:
http://eepurl.com/nmliD

My website:
http://www.suzannamedeiros.com

Facebook:
http://www.facebook.com/AuthorSuzannaMedeiros

Twitter:
http://twitter.com/SuzannaMedeiros

Suzanna

Turn the page to read an excerpt of *Loving the Marquess*—book 1 in the Landing a Lord series.

Loving the Marquess—EXCERPT

She is on the verge of losing everything...
To save her home and keep her two younger siblings safe, Louisa Evans must turn to the head of the family that ruined hers.

He needs an heir...
The Marquess of Overlea is starting to show signs of having inherited the same illness that killed his father and older brother. To prevent the marquisate from falling into the hands of an unscrupulous cousin, Overlea must secure an heir before that illness also claims him.

But he is determined not to be the father of that heir...
Overlea's plan is simple — marry the practical, yet desperate, Miss Evans and hold Louisa to her promise to provide him with an heir. But he waits until after they are married to tell his wife that he intends to have another man father that heir. His careful plan becomes complicated by an almost desperate need to claim Louisa for himself and an outside threat that proves even more dangerous than anticipated.

SUZANNA MEDEIROS

LOUISA HAD NOWHERE else to turn. She'd tried unsuccessfully to find more sewing to take in or to think of some other way to pay Edward Manning the rent he demanded. His suggested alternative was too repulsive to contemplate, let alone accept, and she wouldn't allow him to approach Catherine with his vile proposition.

In a moment of frustration she'd almost told her brother about their landlord's visit. The temptation to have someone with whom she could share this burden was great. She knew, though, that John wouldn't have been able to help, and he was brash enough to do something foolish like challenge Edward to a duel for the proposition he'd made. She couldn't allow that to happen.

She brought the horse she'd borrowed from a neighbor to a stop at the end of the drive and looked across the manicured gardens that spread out before Overlea Manor. Their former home, while respectable in size, was not nearly as grand as the house before her now—three stories in height, two wings sweeping out at the sides, and an impressive portico that rose up to the roofline, all in a rich honey-colored stone. She could only stare at it in wonder, the knowledge that she was completely out of her depth solidifying.

Asking for Overlea's assistance had been the only path open to her. She'd managed to maintain her equanimity during the ride, but now that she was here, her heartbeat quickened. She took a deep breath in a vain attempt to quell her nerves before starting down the drive to the front of the house. When she dismounted, a groom was already headed toward her. She smiled as she handed him the reins.

Back straight, feigning a confidence she was far from feeling, she turned and proceeded up the short stairway to the main entrance. She paused at the top, smoothing a hand over the dark blue skirt of her riding habit. The style was more than a few years out of date now, but there was no point in having a habit in the current style when they didn't even own a horse.

She took another deep breath before lifting the heavy brass knocker and letting it fall. The door was opened immediately by a footman. He looked at her and then glanced beyond. She could see him stiffen when he realized she was unattended. She could only imagine what he must be thinking.

"I am here to see Lord Overlea."

The footman did not bother to hide his disapproval. "The marquess is not in."

He was actually going to close the door on her. Out of sheer desperation, Louisa stepped into the doorway. He would have to physically remove her if he wanted her gone.

"Could you please tell him that Louisa Evans is here to see him?"

She was surprised when his demeanor changed almost instantly. He opened the door wider and stepped back to allow her to enter, all solicitousness now.

"Of course, Miss Evans."

He led her to the drawing room and retreated, closing the door behind him.

Louisa drew in a shaky breath. She'd crossed the first barrier, gaining entrance, but her nerves were still unsettled. The toughest part lay ahead. Asking Overlea for assistance she wasn't certain he would provide. Edward Manning was, after all, his cousin, and given the marquess's reputation he might see nothing wrong with the arrangement Edward had proposed. It was, after all, very common for men of their stature to have mistresses.

She wondered if Overlea had a mistress and found the idea bothered her more than she cared to admit.

Her thoughts were so full of her upcoming

meeting with Overlea that she barely took in her elegant surroundings. She perched on the edge of a cream-colored settee and it took all her focus to keep from fidgeting. As the minutes passed, she found herself growing more anxious. She had been waiting a full quarter of an hour before it occurred to her that Overlea might refuse to see her.

She waited another quarter hour before deciding to seek out the footman. She had just reached the drawing room door when it swung open. Startled, she took a step back.

She'd thought the Marquess of Overlea a handsome man before, but the last time she'd seen him, his clothes had been rumpled from a night of tossing and turning and dark stubble had covered his jaw. He had seemed approachable then. Now, clean-shaven and impeccably dressed, he took her breath away. He wore a coat of deep green that stretched across shoulders that seemed broader now, a waistcoat in a lighter shade of that same color, and fawn buckskins that molded to his muscled thighs and disappeared into boots she suspected were the same ones she remembered removing from him. She was acutely conscious, as she had not been before, of the difference in their stations.

That Overlea was surprised to see her was evident, especially as she was alone. He couldn't know, then, that her reputation was already on the verge of being ruined. That she could very well find herself with no alternative than to accept Edward's proposition if he refused to help her.

"Miss Evans," he said, inclining his head.

She acknowledged his greeting but found herself unable to speak for a moment.

"Please," he said, indicating the settee she had abandoned, "make yourself comfortable."

She sat and watched as he settled himself into a chair opposite her.

"I would ring for tea, but I sense this is not a social call."

"No," she said, before lapsing into silence again. Now that she was here she didn't know how to begin. How could she tell him what his cousin had proposed?

"You appear well today, my lord," she said in an attempt to stall the inevitable uncomfortable conversation. "I assume that your illness has passed?"

"Yes," he said.

His posture was stiff and it was clear he didn't wish to discuss it. She had no alternative but to get straight to the reason for her visit.

"I know you weren't expecting to see me so soon."

"I hadn't expected to see you at all." He shifted forward in his chair, a slight frown pulling at the corners of his mouth, and continued. "You will excuse me for being direct, but what could possibly have happened in the past two days to bring you here? You left me with the impression that you didn't wish to have further contact with me or my family."

She resisted the urge to squirm under his intent gaze.

"It must be quite serious for you to come here unescorted. I thought I would be dealing with your brother, if anyone."

"My brother and sister cannot know I came to see you."

His eyebrows rose at that. His gaze never left her as he leaned back in his chair.

"I've had a visit from your cousin."

"Mary?" he asked, his confusion evident.

She shook her head.

"No, your cousin, Edward Manning."

His frowned. "Why would that bring you here? Are you not his tenant?"

"Not precisely." She hesitated a moment before

continuing. "How much do you know about what happened between my father and your uncle?"

"A fair bit," Overlea replied, his features shuttered.

She was grateful to be spared having to relay the details of what had transpired all those years ago.

"After... well, after what happened, we moved from our old house to where we now live. I suppose after everything he'd taken from us your uncle decided to show us some mercy." She failed to hide the note of bitterness in her voice. "The cottage is one of the larger ones on the estate. I remember my father being worried about the rent now that he didn't have the income from the estate, but your uncle allowed us to live there without having to pay it."

"And now?"

From his almost unnatural stillness, it was clear he suspected what she was about to say.

"Your cousin has informed me that we are to start paying rent immediately."

"And you cannot afford it."

"No," she said, her voice barely above a whisper.

It was several moments before Overlea replied. "Why are you here, Miss Evans? I know you're not here for charity. Would you like me to speak to Edward? Convince him to give you more time? Or perhaps to continue to allow you to remain in your home under the same conditions as when you father was alive? If that's the case, I'm afraid I'll have to disappoint you. I don't have that much influence over my cousin's actions."

She would have to tell him everything. The subject was already an uncomfortable one, but the kiss she and Overlea had shared on that morning after he woke in her room made it even more so. Keeping silent, however, might have grave consequences. Especially for Catherine.

"There is something else," she said, her embarrassment acute. Unable to broach the subject just yet, she stood and walked over to the window. She gazed out at the perfectly manicured grounds for a full minute before taking a deep breath and turning to face him again. Overlea stood, but he didn't say anything, giving her the time she needed. She was grateful for that. "Your cousin did offer me an alternative to paying rent. One that would involve using a currency of a different, much more unpalatable sort."

It took him only a moment to catch her meaning. He scowled and swore softly, but she continued before he could say anything. "John and Catherine know nothing about this, and they must never hear of it. John is hotheaded enough to do something foolish. And Catherine—" Her voice hitched. "He offered to approach her directly and make her the same offer if I refuse."

"Surely she would never agree to such a thing. Not if you speak to her first and give her your support."

"Mama died in childbed during Catherine's birth. A part of her believes she is responsible for the series of events that led us to where we are today. That Papa never would have fallen into your uncle's trap if she'd never been born and Mama hadn't died. Papa never would have turned to drinking, never would have gambled away the estate and our home. Of course," she added, rushing to reassure him lest he think she shared that belief, "Catherine is not to blame for our father's actions, but she might accept your cousin's offer as a way of atoning for all that has happened."

His dark eyes settled on her for what seemed an eternity. She squirmed, uncomfortable being the sole subject of that inscrutable gaze. Finally, he spoke.

"I believe I can help you."

Intense relief washed over her and she had to close her eyes for an instant. She started to thank him, but his words stopped her.

"You may want to hear my conditions first."

An icy finger of dread snaked up her spine. Had she made a mistake in coming here? Was it possible he was as despicable as his cousin?

"Perhaps you should be seated for this."

She stiffened. "That is quite all right. I am comfortable here."

She threw a hasty glance at the door, wondering at her chances for escape, but realized she was being foolish. This man had spent a considerable amount of time under her roof and he'd had several opportunities to make unwanted advances. Other than the one kiss they had shared when he'd woken and mistaken their relationship, an action for which he had later apologized, he had been circumspect in his attentions.

Nevertheless, she shivered when he approached her. His movements were smooth, almost predatory. There was no hint of the caution with which he had moved on that other occasion.

He stopped a few feet from her. She couldn't make out what thoughts lurked behind his dark, intent gaze, but she sensed he was coming to a decision. She didn't have to wait long for him to reach it.

"You require my assistance and I am inclined to

offer it to you, but I have something to ask of you first. Without your agreement, I fear I will be unable to help you."

Louisa couldn't believe what she was hearing. He was about to make her the same offer Edward had made. She was disappointed. For some reason she'd expected better of him.

He was silent for a moment, as if he were choosing his words carefully. When he finally spoke, they were the last she expected to hear.

"I need a wife."

ABOUT THE AUTHOR

Suzanna Medeiros was born and raised in Toronto, Canada. Her love for the written word led her to pursue a degree in English Literature from the University of Toronto. She went on to earn a Bachelor of Education degree, but graduated at a time when no teaching jobs were available. After working at a number of interesting places, including a federal inquiry, a youth probation office, and the Office of the Fire Marshal of Ontario, she decided to pursue her first love—writing.

Suzanna is married to her own hero and is the proud mother of twin daughters. She is an avowed romantic who enjoys spending her days writing love stories.

She would like to thank her parents for showing her that love at first sight and happily ever after really do exist

40627589R00088

Made in the USA
San Bernardino, CA
24 October 2016